Little Grey Rabbit

THE KNOT SQUIRREL TIED

Little Grey Rabbit

THE KNOT SQUIRREL TIED

By Alison Uttley
Pictures by Margaret Tempest

templar
books

ONE MORNING Rat came to his door and gazed up and down with a weary eye. Then he slowly hobbled out to the hazel spinney and made a crutch to help himself along.

Mrs Rat shut the door after him.

"Alas!" she sighed. "It hasn't been the same since he stole the food from Grey Rabbit's house, and that impudent Squirrel tied a knot in his tail."

Rat crept along under the shadow of the wall. No longer could he scamper with his tail rippling behind him. Now it dragged in the heavy knot which Squirrel had tied to remind him of his wickedness. No longer could he thieve or hunt.

"Every day I get thinner and thinner, I never can get a really good dinner," he moaned.

He thought of this as he sidled along by the wall. At last he reached the farm, and he climbed up the narrow stair into the hen house. He knew the Speckledy Hen had laid an egg, for he had heard her boasting to all the world.

Rat crept to the nests. In one of them lay the big brown egg, which had the golden yolk he loved so much. He tucked it under his body, but when he started downstairs the knot in his tail caught in the doorway, and Rat overbalanced.

At that moment the Speckledy Hen looked up.

"My egg! Oh! My dear egg!" she shrieked.

Rat struggled to get free and dropped the egg.

It rolled down the stairway and spilt on the ground and Rat rushed to safety.

"So near and yet so far," he groaned, as he rubbed his sore shins and rested in a hole in the wall. Then he buckled his belt more tightly and slouched around the corner.

Rat crept into the barn where bags of meal stood in a corner. Here was a lucky find! He gnawed a hole in one sack, and had just started to eat the sweet delicious grain, when in his excitement he moved clumsily, and the knot in his tail thumped on the boards.

Into the barn came the farmyard cat, with her eyes gleaming, and her large mouth wide open.

What a race Rat had for the door!

How his tail thumped behind him! He only just got safely away, with his coat torn.

"That was a near squeak," said he, and sat down to think. "Hedgehog is a kindly soul. I'll have a talk with him at milking time."

He waited all afternoon till Hedgehog came trotting across the field with his milk pails jingling-jangling on the chains.

The Rat watched Hedgehog milk a cow and turn away with the warm milk frothing in his little pails. He licked his lips hungrily and then stepped softly after.

Old Hedgehog heard the thump of the tail, and exclaimed without turning round, "Is that you, Rat? Keep away from my milk pails."

"Mr Hedgehog," said Rat humbly. "A word with you, Sir."

Hedgehog put down the pails and waited.

   "I never get anything to eat nowadays,"
said Rat.
   "What do you want me to do, Rat?
I'll give you a drink of milk if you like."

The kindly Hedgehog held out a pail and Rat drank it all up with eager gulps.

"Please, kind Hedgehog," whined Rat. "Give me some advice. Everyone knows how wise you are."

"First time I've been called wise," said Old Hedgehog.

"How can I get the knot undone, Hedgehog?" asked Rat.

"Let me see what I can do. My fingers are all thumbs, but I'll use my prickles."

"Oh! Oh! Oh-oo ooh!" squealed Rat as Hedgehog tugged at the knot with his spikes.

"I can't undo it, Rat. Clever fingers fastened it," said he. "Go and ask Mole's advice."

Rat tramped up the field. There was Mole's house, with Mole digging in his garden. He put down his spade.

"Good afternoon, Rat," said he. "May I ask what brings you here?"

"Please, Mole, can you untie the knot in my tail?" asked the Rat in a tiny, sad little voice. "Hedgehog sent me to you, for he couldn't loosen it."

Without a word Mole trotted indoors, and returned with a bowl of soup and a slice of bread.

"Eat this," said he. "Then I will look at it."

Rat thanked him and gobbled up the food.

Then Mole seized the knot with his long pink fingers and struggled and tugged, but still the knot wouldn't come undone.

"It's Squirrel's tying," said he, "but I don't think even her clever fingers could undo this knot. The only one who can help you is Wise Owl."

"I daren't go to him," said Rat.

"Take him a present," replied Mole.

"I am so poor, I have nothing," said Rat to himself as he turned away.

He put his hand in his pocket and brought out a ragged handkerchief and a bone.

"I haven't even a knife, but my teeth are as sharp as a razor. They will do the job."

He sat down on a log and gnawed at the bone. He bit a piece off here, and a slip off there, and a snippet from one end, working away, polishing and rubbing as he went. Night came before he had finished, and he took home his carving.

"Have you brought any food, Rat?" asked his wife, when she opened the door.

"Nothing, wife," said Rat, "but tomorrow I'm going to see Wise Owl." He showed his wife his carving and she sat admiring it.

It was a little white ship with rigging and
sails, and tiny portholes. At the prow was a
seagull with outstretched wings.

The next day Rat set off with his ship. The billowing sails were nearly transparent with his polishing, and the ropes were like cobwebs.

On his way to Wise Owl's he had to pass Little Grey Rabbit's cottage. Delicious smells came from the window, and Rat crept up to see what was being cooked. He didn't want to get to Owl's house till dusk, so there was plenty of time.

Little Grey Rabbit and Squirrel were making tartlets. Grey Rabbit rolled out the pastry with her little rolling pin, and Squirrel lined the patty pans ready for the raspberry jam.

"Grey Rabbit, Grey Rabbit," called Hare, running up the garden path and bursting into the kitchen.

Rat hid under the juniper bush and Hare passed him without noticing.

"Haymaking has begun!" said he. "Can we all go and play in the hayfield? The grass will be hay tomorrow with this sunshine."

"Oh, let's," cried Grey Rabbit, and she waved her rolling pin excitedly. "We'll invite Mole and Hedgehog and Fuzzypeg to join us, and we'll have tea in the hayfield tomorrow evening."

"I'll make some treacle toffee to take with us," said Hare. He took a saucepan and measured out butter and treacle and sugar. He stirred it over the fire, getting in Squirrel's way, and knocking over the flour bin.

Soon a sweet smell came into the room.

Little Grey Rabbit put her tartlets in the oven, and Hare set his toffee on the windowsill to cool. Then they all went out in the garden and sat among the flowers, sipping lemonade and fanning themselves with leaves.

Rat crept up to the back door, and looked into the cosy kitchen. He knew his way about.

"Ah!" he sighed, and he dragged his unwilling tail over the doorway. "I'm safe for a few minutes."

He crouched down by the fire, and sniffed the savoury smells of raspberry tartlets which came from the oven. He opened the oven door and poked his nose in the hot jam.

"Oh!" he squeaked in a muffled voice. "Too hot!"

He dipped the tip of his tail in the cooling
toffee, but that was too hot, also. Through the
open window he heard the three friends make
plans for the picnic.

"There's my chance," said Rat. "I'll come
along tomorrow and see what I can find."

He looked again at his little ship, white as ivory, and pretty as a picture. Then he shuffled out of the house, and went through the wood to Wise Owl's house in the great beech tree.

He rang the little silver bell which hung from the door, and the sleepy bird came to see who wanted him in the daylight.

"Rat!" said he gruffly. "What do you want?"

"I've brought you a present, Wise Owl." Rat spoke in a trembling voice.

Wise Owl sat waiting, with his large round eyes staring at the unfortunate rat, while Rat fumbled in his pocket and brought out the little ship.

"Hm-m," said Wise Owl, flying down. "A nice bit of carving. Pity you don't do more work, Rat. Why not try to work instead of to thieve?"

"Please, Wise Owl, will you unknot my tail?" asked Rat humbly. "I am as thin as a leaf, and no one is clever enough to unknot me."

Owl hummed to himself and turned the tiny bone ship over and over.

"I'm afraid you are still a thief, Rat. What about Speckledy Hen's egg? What about the farmer's corn? Where did that jam come from, which I see on your nose? And that treacle toffee on the end of your tail?"

Rat fidgeted uneasily. What keen eyes had Owl!

"The knot will stay tied until you turn over a new leaf, Rat!"

Owl shut his door and went back to his
library, holding the little ship in his claws.
He took down his book on sailing ships.

"Quite correct in every detail," said he.

Rat hobbled painfully back through the wood, turning all the green leaves he could reach, but still his tail remained knotted. However, he felt happier, for he had made something, and Owl had looked pleased with it.

The next day, as usual, he paid his visit to the farmyard, to see what he could pilfer. He walked up to the hen roost and there was the Speckledy Hen's latest egg. Rat looked at it with longing eyes. Speckledy Hen was a good-natured silly creature. He would leave her egg. There would be raspberry tartlets at Grey Rabbit's house.

He turned away and started to go down the stair. Was it imagination? He felt a loosening in his tail. The knot thumped less noisily as he slid down.

The Speckledy Hen ran shrieking to her precious egg. There it was, safe and sound! She couldn't understand. Had Rat turned over a new leaf?

Rat went into the barn. There was litter on the floor, and he seized a bunch of twigs. Up and down the stones he went, sweeping softly, with scarcely a glance at the meal bag, until the floor was clean.

Then he went up to the sack and gazed at its bulging sides. A pity to mess up the floor again! There would be raspberry tartlets waiting for him. He turned away, and another little hitch in his tail seemed to be loosened.

He went to Hedgehog's house under the hedge.

"Can I do any little thing for you, Hedgehog?" he asked.

Old Hedgehog stared. "Do you mean a little burglary?" he asked.

"No. I'll help you carry your milk pails to the neighbours," said Rat. "Try me."

So Hedgehog trusted him with the milk for the Red Squirrel.

Rat took the milk to the Red Squirrel's door, and knocked gently. He filled the jug at the foot of the tree, and turned away.

Rat walked through the fields. Both his heart and his tail felt lighter, and when he got back to Hedgehog's house, there was a hunch of bread and cheese waiting for him. Fuzzypeg peeped round the corner. Rat put his hand in his pocket and brought out a dozen oak apples, which he gave to the astonished little hedgehog for marbles.

As evening came there were sounds of gaiety in the hayfield. Squirrel and Little Grey Rabbit in blue sun bonnets were raking the hay, and Hare was piling it up into haycocks.

Hedgehog and Fuzzypeg came to help and tossed it with their prickles. Then Mole joined them, with a little hayfork which he had made.

Rat stood looking at the happy scene – an outsider. He was on his way to Grey Rabbit's house, where he hoped to find the raspberry tartlets waiting for him. He wouldn't be caught this time! He knew his way about, and Squirrel was safe for an hour or two.

Then he noticed the feast spread out under the hedge, not far from him.

There it lay, in the shade of the foxgloves, with no one to guard it!

There was a little white cloth and on it a basket filled with the raspberry tartlets! So it was of no use to go to the house, for the food was here!

There were nut leaves laden with wild strawberries and raspberries, and a jug full of cream. There was crab apple jelly and sloe jam, little green lettuces and radishes like rosebuds, and a big plum cake, and the treacle toffee!

Rat's mouth watered. He stared so hard at the plum cake that he felt he could taste its delicious sugary crust.

Then he turned away and walked home.

A great pink cloud lay in the sky, and swifts cut across the blue air. Rat gazed up at the sky, at the birds, so light and free, and at that moment he felt light and free too. The last knot in his tail had come undone. He was a happy Rat, loosened from his fetters, and he ran home to tell his wife, whisking his tail around his head.

"I saw Rat staring at our feast," confided Grey Rabbit to the others as they sat among the foxgloves. "He didn't touch a thing."

"Rat helped to carry my milk today, and swept the barn clean," said Old Hedgehog.

"Rat gave me some marbles," cried Fuzzypeg.

"I wonder if Wise Owl gave him some good advice," mused the Mole.

The next morning Rat came to Little Grey Rabbit's house. He carried a pair of shears and a scythe and he walked with a quick light step.

"Can I gather your firewood, Grey Rabbit?" said he. "Can I mow your lawn, or cut your hedge?"

"Why! The knot has gone from your tail, Rat!" exclaimed Grey Rabbit. "Who untied it, Rat?"

"It came undone by itself," replied Rat modestly. "I'm not a thief any more. I understand now what Wise Owl meant when he told me to turn over a new leaf. I shall work for my living."

He took up his shears and cut the hedge, making peacocks and balls and ships. He mowed the lawn as smooth as silk, and he pulled up every tiny weed in the garden.

He went in the wood to gather sticks, and as he passed under Owl's tree, the wise bird looked out.

"Ho! Ho!" he hooted. "A reformed Rat. The knot is not! A skillful Rat! An artist! Go on with the good work, Rat, and bring me another present someday. I shall be honoured to accept it."

The Rat blushed through his dusky skin with pride, but he went on gathering sticks. When he had a great bundle he carried it to the door of the little house.

Rat went home with his wages in his pocket, a respectable working animal.

"I'm going to carve something else," said he to his wife. "You've never seen anything like what I'm going to make!" He sat down at the table with his little white bone, and began to carve – but that is a secret for another time!

A TEMPLAR BOOK

This edition first published in the UK in 2018 by Templar Publishing,
an imprint of Kings Road Publishing, part of the Bonnier Publishing Group,
The Plaza, 535 King's Road, London, SW10 0SZ
www.bonnierpublishing.com

Original edition first published in the UK in 1937
by William Collins Sons & Co Ltd

This edition edited by Susan Dickinson and Ruth Symons
Additional design by Nathalie Eyraud

1 3 5 7 9 10 8 6 4 2

ISBN 978-1-78370-842-0

Printed in China